Just Visiting

by Becky Cheston
illustrated by Erin Eitter Kono

Harcourt

SCHOOL PUBLISHERS

Requests for permission to make copies of any part of the work should be addressed to School Permissions and Copyrights, Harcourt, Inc., 6277 Sea Harbor Drive, Orlando, Florida 32887–6777. Fax: 407-345-2418.

HARCOURT and the Harcourt Logo are trademarks of Harcourt, Inc., registered in the United States of America and/or other jurisdictions.

Printed in China

ISBN 10: 0-15-351675-5
ISBN 13: 978-0-15-351675-7

Ordering Options
ISBN 10: 0-15-351215-6 (Grade 5 Advanced Collection)
ISBN 13: 978-0-15-351215-5 (Grade 5 Advanced Collection)
ISBN 10: 0-15-358158-1 (package of 5)
ISBN 13: 978-0-15-358158-8 (package of 5)

5 6 7 8 9 10   468 12 11 10 09

How could I be mad at Arwen? Becca thought. With a giant sigh, she sank to a sitting position on the hardwood floor. In front of her, framed by the fireplace, sat Arwen, her dog. Arwen was covered in soft, golden curls. At the moment, Arwen was panting peacefully, staring at Becca with adoring, long-lashed eyes.

"Oh, Ari," said Becca, burying her face in the dog's neck. Still, even the hug couldn't banish Becca's frustration over having to rush home from school today to walk Arwen.

In fact, this negative feeling was only the first stop in a whole journey of resentments. The second stop was Station Joel. Sure, the whole family had been elated when her big brother made the soccer team. Did anyone realize, however, what this meant for her? Walking Arwen after school had been Joel's job. Now she had to skip out on her friends and rush right home. She'd already missed volleyball, dance tips from Gina's big sister, and some important gossip. What else had gone on without her?

Becca curled up against Arwen's side and got back on the frustration train. Next stop: the twins. Of course, she adored them. In April, when Mom and Dad had brought them home from the hospital, she'd fallen instantly in love. These were the same baby girls, however, who kept Mom home during the afternoon. Home, and not walking the dog. Just then, the door banged open. Arwen jumped to her feet, spilling Becca onto the floor.

"Ari! How's my good dog? How's the best dog in the whole wide world?" Joel scrubbed Arwen's head with his knuckles as the dog stood on her hind legs to greet him. "Hey, Becca? How goes it?" Joel, dressed in blue shorts and a white mesh soccer shirt, had released Arwen, and was now bouncing a soccer ball from one knee to the other in the yard.

"It goes the same way it always does. Finish school, miss a fun activity, walk dog," said Becca while she walked out the door.

"Did you work at teaching her to fetch?" asked Joel.

"She's almost two," said Becca. "If she was going to show an interest in fetching, she would have done it by now."

Joel kicked his soccer ball lightly over to the dog. "Stop the goal, girl! Jump on it!" Arwen just stood there looking up at him, wagging her tail and smiling. "No soccer, no fetching . . . Just what do you like, Ari?" He scratched her behind the ears and turned to Becca. "How was the walk?"

Becca rolled her eyes. Today's walk was pretty much the same as yesterday's walk, which was no different from the day before that. Joel walked back into the house, grabbed an orange and a plate, and sat at the small, round table. Arwen pranced in behind him, her toenails clicking on the floor. Becca followed, recounting what had happened during her usual dog walk.

"I can only take her around the block, you know," she said. "Mom doesn't want me crossing the street, so the park's not an option."

"This week, Carmine has been outside painting the Ramirez house," said Becca.

Every day now, Carmine stood waiting at the fence in his painter's overalls. When Arwen approached, the dog dashed through the open gate and flew into his arms. Carmine was a student at the local college who lived with the Ramirez family and missed his own dog. The first day he saw Arwen, he asked, "What kind of mutt is she?"

"She is not a mutt," Becca said. "She's a 'golden doodle'. It's sort of a new breed—a cross between a poodle and a golden retriever."

Today Carmine convinced Becca to let him play with Arwen for a few minutes. Then he thanked her over and over again, with great fervor. "It's the high point of my day," he said, waving good-bye.

As they continued down the sidewalk, Becca could hear the racket coming from the Simpson's yard next door. Fred and Jenna Simpson had four kids, all under the age of six. At this time of day, they played noisily outside, riding tricycles, fighting over toys, and gouging sticks into the dirt. At least one child was always crying—and today was no different.

Arwen, who loved children, pulled Becca to a stop in front of the Simpson's low, chain-link fence. Mrs. Simpson was drooping with fatigue, crouched on one knee, a sobbing toddler encircled in each arm. Calmly, she looked back and forth as each little boy tried to explain how the other had wronged

him. Becca didn't get how Mrs. Simpson understood them or how she could so patiently assuage their distress. Arwen, though, seemed to know precisely what to do. Standing on her hind legs, she leaned over the fence and licked each boy once on the hand. It was like an electric switch that instantly stopped the crying. Then one toddler produced a big, baby belly laugh, which set his brother off into a fit of giggles. The other two children ran over.

"Can Arwen come in the yard?" asked the oldest.

"Sure," Mrs. Simpson said, smiling. Becca let Arwen lie on the grass for a few minutes as the children petted and hugged her, calling out, "Ah-win! Ah-win!"

"That dog is a lifesaver," Mrs. Simpson said.

When Becca finally led Arwen out of the yard, the children stood at the fence, their tiny fingers poking through the wire. Becca could now see the end of the street, where Hennigan's Grocery sat on the corner. Sometimes Mr. Hennigan saw them through the window, and if he wasn't busy, he fed Arwen a hot dog from the glass-enclosed rotisserie.

Just before the store stood the Orthopedic Rehabilitation Clinic. A nurse had once explained to Becca that people came here to recover from injuries or surgeries involving bones. If the weather was decent, patients would sit outside socializing or quietly watching the street. Sometimes a physical therapist accompanied a patient up and down the front path.

Arwen always dragged Becca onto the clinic grounds to visit people. This week, Arwen and Becca saw a twelve-year-old boy, a smattering of adults of various ages, a young football player, and a physical therapist named Lucille. The boy, whose name was Carter, looked desolate sitting in a wheelchair apart from the others. His left leg, which he'd broken in a hiking accident, was propped up. Yesterday, he'd told Becca that he was supposed to be learning to walk in his cast with a cane, but it was very hard. Becca saw his eyes brighten when he spotted Arwen strutting up the path.

First, however, Arwen stopped where Lucille sat with a woman with one arm in a sling. "There's that lovely dog again!" the woman exclaimed.

"Hello, Becca," said Lucille. The clinic staffer wore a freshly ironed, immaculate white coat. "Have you met Bronson?" She introduced Becca to the football player, who was practicing getting around on crutches. He petted Arwen as he questioned Becca about the breed. From the corner of her eye, Becca could see Carter trying to move his chair onto the path toward Arwen. The wheelchair, however, would not cooperate. Suddenly, Carter reached around to the back of his chair and grabbed his cane.

Carter stood, wincing in anticipation of certain pain. As he braced himself with the cane, though, he seemed surprised that he felt so little discomfort. Gingerly, he hopped along the path until he reached the little cluster of people who were fussing over Arwen.

"We were going to come over there and see you," Becca told him.

Carter shrugged. "That's okay. I'm supposed to be up and walking anyway."

Becca stayed and let Arwen visit with the patients for a while. Finally, when it was time for Becca to head home, Lucille walked her and Arwen down to the sidewalk. "Well!" she exclaimed. "I've been working hard for days to get that boy up and walking. Then along comes Arwen, and she gets him on his feet without even trying!"

Later that day, Becca sat doing her homework at the kitchen table while her mom fed the twins, Claire and Sophie. Arwen lay on the floor between the two high chairs, waiting for food to drop. Before long, Joel bounded in to hover in front of the open refrigerator.

He cut up a banana and set half the pieces in front of each twin. Claire began pounding her tray in excitement. Sophie copied her.

Then, Joel took a packet of lunch meat from the refrigerator and shut the door. As he placed a few pieces of turkey on a plate, Arwen rose and trotted over to him. "Figures. Hey, that's your thing, Ari: food."

"You're just figuring that out now?" teased Mom. "She's a dog, you silly boy." Mom bustled around, fetching crackers and pouring juice into matching sip cups.

Becca looked up from her books. "That's mean, Joel. Arwen's not just about food. She does other stuff."

"Oh, really? Name one thing."

Just then, Claire squealed and flung her cracker to the floor. Arwen dove for it, swallowing it in one bite, then licking every last crumb off the floor. Next, it was Sophie's turn to toss a cracker. Now both girls were whining and pointing at the cracker box. "All right," said Mom, giving them each one more. "No more throwing, okay? No throwing."

As soon as the girls got their new crackers, they threw them to Arwen and screamed for more. "That's it!" said Joel. "I'm out of here." He left with his plate of turkey as the twins began to cry.

"Snack is over, girls," said Mom, cleaning the high chairs. By the time she finished wiping the twins' faces, they were red-cheeked, angry, and sobbing at maximum volume. Becca sighed, shut her notebook, and lifted Claire out of her highchair. Mom took Sophie, and they both sat at the table, trying to comfort the babies.

"What is wrong with them today?" Becca asked.

"They hardly slept," replied Mom, rubbing Sophie between the shoulder blades and whispering. "It seems like they might be old enough to give up their afternoon nap."

"It seems like they need more sleep, not less," said Becca.

"They'll do better once we get into a new routine," said Mom. "I've been thinking. Tomorrow, instead of napping, we'll go for a walk. I'll take Arwen, too. Then you don't have to rush home after school."

"Really?" Becca had not expected this. For some reason, it made her uneasy. "Which way will you go?"

"To the park."

Becca stood. "Maybe we should put them in the playpen," she said, carrying Claire into the living room.

Her mother followed with Sophie. "Are you okay, Becca?"

"Sure, Mom. I think I should probably go upstairs and get some work done." Becca didn't feel okay, though. As she climbed the stairs to her room, she tried to figure out why.

Becca had been sitting at her desk for a full ten minutes before she realized that she'd left her schoolbooks in the kitchen. She'd get them later—there was no way she could concentrate on homework now. A worry had traveled from the back of her mind to the front, where she could look at it head on. If her mom took the twins to the park, she'd be walking in the other direction. Why did this bother her so? She'd finally gotten her wish—she was free to be with her friends after school. Why was she worrying instead of celebrating?

The sound of a creaking door made Becca look up. There was Arwen's coal black nose, poking into the room. "You coming to visit me, girl?" The dog trotted into the room and put her head in Becca's lap. Joel was wrong about Arwen—she did have a "thing." It had taken Becca a while to understand what her neighbors already knew: Arwen liked to visit her neighbors. What's more, they seemed to depend on her.

As she realized this, Becca knew she wouldn't be meeting her friends after school tomorrow. Arwen needed to go visiting—and she couldn't do it alone.

14

Think Critically

1. Why does Becca have to walk Arwen after school?

2. The author uses the image of a "frustration train" to describe how Becca deals with her resentful feelings about walking Arwen. Is this image effective? Explain why or why not.

3. What is similar about the way both Carter and the Simpson kids react to Arwen?

4. How does Becca react when Mom tells her she no longer has to walk Arwen? What does her reaction reveal about her character?

5. What do you think about how the book portrays the value of "visiting" dogs?

 Social Studies

Ancient Pets Research the history of keeping animals as pets. What kind of pets did people have in ancient times? How did people interact with their pets? Summarize your findings in a few paragraphs.

 School-Home Connection Share this story with a family member. What was their favorite part and why?

Word Count: 2,044